The San Paul GROUP

prese

MW01123281

Q.T. pie ™

in

The Ingredients of a Q.T. Pie

By Stephanie Sanders
Illustrated by Galen T. Pauling

Published by The SanPaul Group, L.L.C., Detroit, Michigan 48219

Library of Congress Catalog Card Number: 99-93770 ISBN: 0-9670875-0-3

Hi, my name is Quintessence T. Pie.

My mama calls me "Q. T. Pie" for short. She says
every girl in the world is a Q. T. Pie even if her name
doesn't begin with Q. If you'd give me a minute or
two, I'll tell you the ingredients of a Q. T. Pie that
makes this statement true.

Take one cup of sugar, one charming smile...

Two eyes that twinkle, one teaspoonful of style...

one tablespoon of grace, add hair of any color,
and a face of any race.

Heaps of imagination to whet the intellect,

Plenty of pride and self-respect,

and a pinch of allspice to create
the most positive attitude.

Take all these ingredients and
mix them up just so...

It's this very special mix of ingredients
that makes us glow.

You see, it's not the crust but the filling inside.
As unique and individual as the stars in the midnight
sky, every girl in the world is a Q. T. Pie.